Hedgehugs

by Lucy Tapper & Steve Wilson

Horace and Hattie are
the very best of friends.

There are so many things
they like to do together.

They like to search for four-leaved
clover in the meadow.

They like to make daisy chains in the shade of the old oak tree.

They like to splash in puddles on the lawn.

And sometimes they like to
have a tea party by the river.

When Horace is busy,
Hattie puts on her tutu and
dances in the bluebells.

When Hattie is busy,
Horace searches for
spiders in the woods.

Horace and Hattie are the very best of friends.

But there is one thing that they cannot do together.

They cannot hug.

They are just too spiky!

They have tried lots of ways to hug.

In winter, they rolled in the snow
until it covered all their prickles.

But the hug was too cold.

In spring, they found some old, hollow logs.

Horace and Hattie squeezed inside.

But the hug was too bumpy.

In summer, they stuck
strawberries on their spikes.

But the hug was too sticky.

In autumn they covered their
prickles in crunchy, crispy leaves.

But the hug was too scratchy.

Poor Horace and Hattie.

Then one day they found
something very interesting.

It was very soft.

Was it a hat?

Horace decided to investigate.

He wriggled
and jiggled
and nibbled.

Then out he **popped**!

Hattie thought Horace
looked very funny.

Then she had an
amazing idea.

Hattie looked at Horace.

Horace looked at Hattie.

They moved **closer** and **closer** and **closer** until . . .

...They hugged!

The hug was just right.

Not cold, not scratchy, not sticky and not bumpy.
It was warm and soft and cuddly and comfy.

A perfect hedgehug.

So, when you see someone wearing odd socks
or next time one of your socks goes missing,
you know what it means.

A hedgehug has happened!

'Hedgehugs'

An original concept by Lucy Tapper and Steve Wilson

© Lucy Tapper and Steve Wilson

Written by Steve Wilson

Illustrated by Lucy Tapper

Published by MAVERICK ARTS PUBLISHING LTD

Studio 3A, City Business Centre, 6 Brighton Road, Horsham, West Sussex, RH13 5BB

© Maverick Arts Publishing Limited January 2014 +44 (0)1403 256941

A CIP catalogue record for this book is available at the British Library.

ISBN 978-1-84886-111-4

Maverick
arts publishing
www.maverickbooks.co.uk

Lucy's World

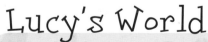

Lucy Tapper is an illustrator, artist and designer. She loves all things beautiful and likes to surround herself with wild flowers, pretty fabrics and colour. Lucy is the creative force behind 'www.lucysworld.co.uk.'

Steve Wilson is the other half of Lucy's World and has a long history in children's TV presenting and writing music, hence his love of words, stories and characters.

Steve and Lucy live in a little cottage in Devon with their two daughters Daisy and Holly.